Spies

and

Pies

The Sound of IE

By Jody Jensen Shaffer

Two spies see pies.

The spies see apple pies.

The spies see cherry pies.

The spies see peach pies.

9

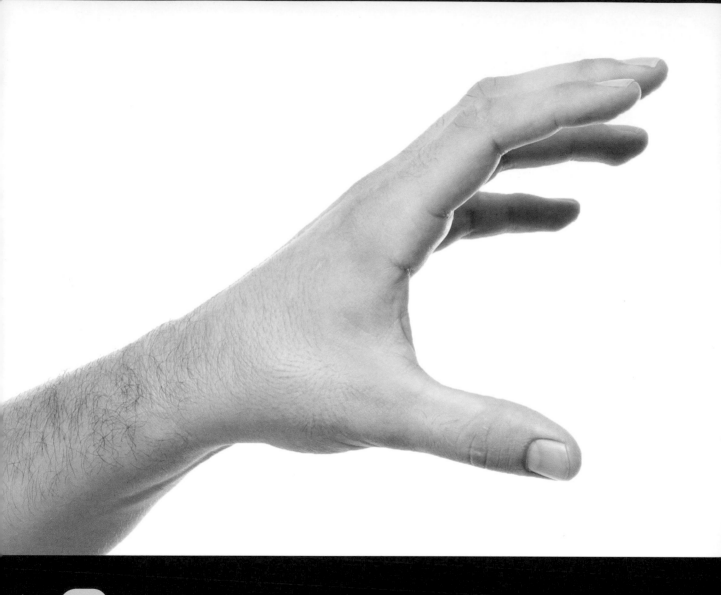

10

The spies want the pies.

The spies tie strings to apple pies.

13

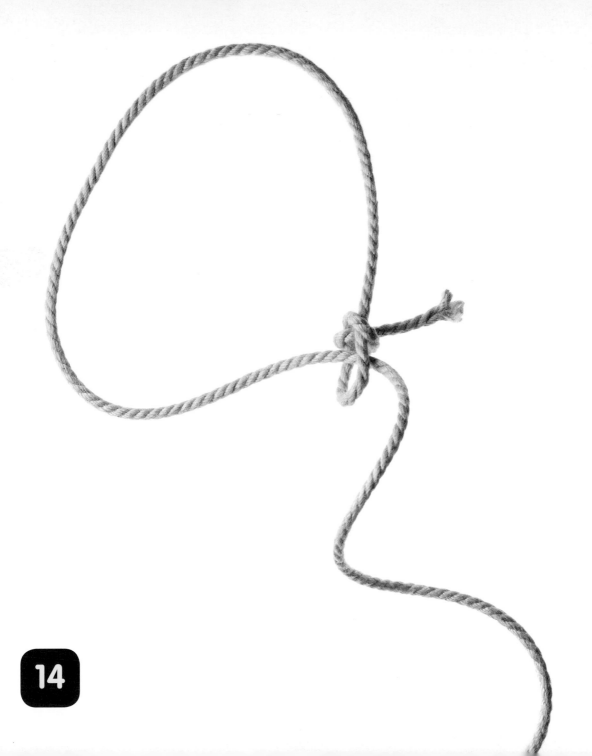

14

The spies tie strings to cherry pies.

The spies tie strings to peach pies.

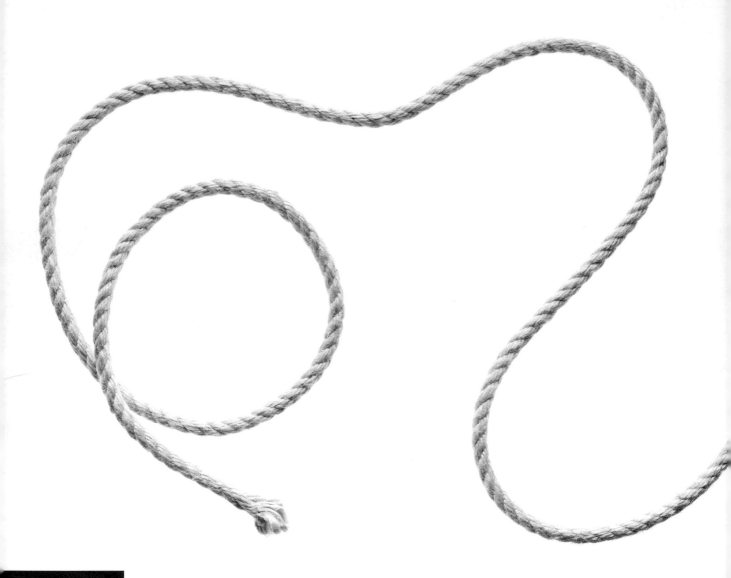

The strings come untied.

Oh well.
The spies tried!

21

Word List:

pies   tried

spies   untied

tie

Note to Caregivers and Educators

The books in this series are based on current research, which supports the idea that our brains are pattern-detectors rather than rules-appliers. This means children learn to read easier when they are taught the familiar spelling patterns found in English. As children encounter more complex words, they have greater success in figuring out these words by using the spelling patterns.

Throughout the series, the texts allow the reader to practice and apply knowledge of the sounds in natural language. The books introduce sounds using familiar onsets and *rimes*, or spelling patterns, for reinforcement.

For example, the word *cat* might be used to present the short "a" sound, with the letter *c* being the onset and "_at" being the rime. This approach provides practice and reinforcement of the short "a" sound, as there are many familiar words made with the "_at" rime.

The stories and accompanying photographs in this series are based on time-honored concepts in children's literature: well-written, engaging texts and colorful, high-quality photographs combine to produce books that children want to read again and again.

Dr. Peg Ballard
Minnesota State University, Mankato

The Child's World®
childsworld.com

Published by The Child's World®
1980 Lookout Drive • Mankato, MN 56003-1705
800-599-READ • www.childsworld.com

PHOTO CREDITS
© Borja Andreu/Shutterstock.com: 10; Daxiao Productions/
Shutterstock.com: 5; FuzzBones/Shutterstock.com:
cover (left spy), 2 (left), 21 (left); getfile/Shutterstock.com:
cover (right spy), 2 (right,) 21 (right); MSPhotographic/
Shutterstock.com: 9; Peter Zijlstra/Shutterstock.com: cover
(pies); Viktoria Hodos/Shutterstock.com: 6; Yeti studio/
Shutterstock.com: 13, 14, 17, 18

ISBN 9781503835412
LCCN 2019944827

Printed in the United States of America

ABOUT THE AUTHOR

Jody Jensen Shaffer has written dozens
of books for children. She also publishes
poetry, stories, and articles in children's
magazines. When she's not writing,
Jody copy edits for children's publishers.
She lives in Missouri.